Little New Kangaroo

to Nina—B.W.

to Paul, Mimi, and Eddie—T.B.

Clarion Books, a Houghton Mifflin Company imprint. 215 Park Avenue South, New York, NY 10003.
Text copyright © 1993 by Bernard Wiseman. Illustrations copyright © 1993 by Theresa Burns.
All rights reserved.
For information about permission to reproduce selections from this book, write to Permissions,
Houghton Mifflin Company, 215 Park Avenue South, New York, NY 10003. Printed in U.S.A. Library of
Congress Cataloging-in-Publication Data. Wiseman, Bernard. Little new kangaroo / by Bernard
Wiseman ; illustrated by Theresa Burns. p. cm . Summary: While riding in his mother's pouch, a
young kangaroo makes friends with four other animals whom he invites to ride with him.
ISBN 0-395-65362-2 [1. Kangaroos–Fiction. 2. Stories in rhyme.] I. Burns, Theresa, ill. II. Title.
PZ8.3.W75Li 1993 [E]–dc20 92-21955 CIP AC

BVG 10 9 8 7 6 5 4 3 2 1

Little New Kangaroo

by Bernard Wiseman

Illustrated by Theresa Burns

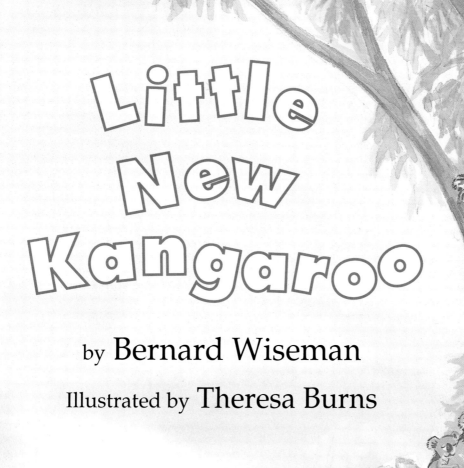

CLARION BOOKS
New York

Little new kangaroo . . .

Mama hops—

out he pops!

He falls down.

He yells, "Ouch!

I fell out of the pouch."

Mama says, "Hold on tight.

Then you will be all right."

Little new kangaroo . . .

Now he knows what to do.

He says, "Look—
look who's there!
A new koala bear!

Hello, friend.
Come inside.
Sit with me.
Take a ride!"
Little new kangaroo
tells the bear what to do.
"Hold on tight!
Hold on tight!
Hold on with all your might!"

Mama hops.
She hops high.
The bear yells, "You can fly!"

They see a bandicoot
eating a piece of fruit.

Little new kangaroo yells,
"Come on—you come, too!
Come inside.
Have a seat,
and give us fruit to eat."
He gives them each a bite.
They tell him, "Hold on tight!"
Mama says, "Please sit still
while I hop up that hill."

Mama hops.
Up they go!
But her hops now are low.
Mama says,
"Puff . . . puff . . . puff.
No more friends!
Three's enough."

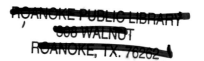

Then they see a wombat.

He is round.

He is fat.

He yells, "Fruit!

I want some.

I love fruit—let me come!"

Mama yells,

"Please—no more!

I cannot carry four!"

Little new kangaroo cries,

"Mama, take him, too!

You are big.

You are strong.

You can take him along!"

Mama gives a big sigh.

She says, "Well . . . I will try."

Mama hops.

Mama sweats.

Oh, how tired Mama gets!

Wombat looks up the hill
and he sees a duckbill.

"There's a duck!" wombat cries.
But he gets a surprise . . .
It has hair on its back
and it does not say quack!
Bandicoot starts to laugh.
He says, "Look—
half and half!"
Mama yells,
"Shame! Shame! Shame!
Platypus is his name!"

Platypus looks so sad
they all feel very bad.
Little new kangaroo
says, "Hello!
How are you?"
Mama says, "Platypus,
climb in here—
come with us."
Mama hops for a while.
Platypus starts to smile.
Mama says,
"Puff . . . I think,
I would like a little drink."

They all drink.
Glup! Glup! Glup!
Mama says, "Hurry up!

It is late.

We must go.

Bedtime is soon, you know."

They all cry, "Let us stay!
We all want time to play."

They play games.
They have fun
till there is no more sun,

no more light . . .
It is dark.
It is night.

Mama cries,

"Climb in fast!

Let us see who is last."

Wombat's last!

They all joke,

"Wombat is a slowpoke!"

They all yawn.
Mama hops . . .
At each home Mama stops.
Parents say, "Be polite.
Wave your paw!
Say good night!"

Little new kangaroo . . .

Soon he is at home, too.

He has made four new friends.

Now he sleeps.

His day ends.